CLIFFHANGER

Jacqueline Wilson

Illustrated by Nick Sharratt

Galaxy

CHIVERS PRESS
BATH

First published in 1995
by
Corgi Yearling
This Large Print edition published by
Chivers Press
by arrangement with
Transworld Publishers Ltd
2000

ISBN 0 7540 6120 5

Cliffhanger was originally written as a two-part drama for the Channel 4 Schools series *Talk, Write and Read*. *Cliffhanger* was produced by Central Television for Channel 4 Schools, first broadcast January 1995

British Library Cataloguing in Publication Data

Wilson, Jacqueline
    Cliffhanger. —Large print ed.
    1. Children's stories   2. Large type books
    I. Title
    823.9'14[J]

ISBN 0-7540-6120-5

Printed and bound in Great Britain by
REDWOOD BOOKS, Trowbridge, Wiltshire

For Tim and Joanna

CLIFFHANGER

The boy Tigers

Giles

Me

Biscuits

POST CARD

Dear Mum and Dad
I am at the Adventure Centre.
Well. You know that. You took
me here.
    I have only been here half an
hour. I am not enjoying it so
far. Not one bit.
        With love from
                Tim
    xxxxxxxx to Mum
            x to Dad

Mr and Mrs R. Parsons,
10 Rainbow Street,
Didcot,
Oxon

1st

CHAPTER ONE

I *knew* I'd hate it. I kept telling and telling Dad. But he wouldn't listen to me. He never does.

'I like the sound of this adventure holiday for children,' said Dad, pointing to the advert in the paper. 'Abseiling, canoeing, archery, mountain biking . . .'

'Sounds a bit dangerous to me,' said Mum.

I didn't say anything. I went on watching telly.

'How about it, Tim?' said Dad. 'What about an adventure holiday, eh?'

'You can't be serious! Tim's much too young,' said Mum.

I still didn't say anything. I went on watching telly. But my heart had started thumping under my T-shirt.

'He's nine, for goodness sake!' said Dad.

'But he's young for his age,' said Mum.

I still didn't say anything. I went on

Walter Bear

watching telly. I stared hard at the screen, wishing there was some way I could step inside.

'Tim?' said Dad.

I didn't look round quickly enough.

'Tim! Stop watching television!' Dad shouted.

I jumped.

'Don't shout at him like that,' said Mum.

'I'm not shouting,' Dad shouted. He took a deep breath. He turned his lips up into a big smile. 'Now, Tim—you'd like to go on an adventure holiday, wouldn't you?'

'He'd hate it,' said Mum.

'Let him answer for himself,' said Dad. He had hold of me by the shoulders.

'I—I don't really like adventures much, Dad,' I said.

Dad went on smiling, but I think he wanted to give my shoulders a shake.

'Well, what do you like, Tim?' asked Dad.

'Watching telly,' I said.

Dad snorted.

'And drawing and reading and doing puzzles,' said Mum. 'And he comes top in all his lessons at school. Apart from games. You know he's hopeless at sport.'

'Only because he doesn't give it a try,' said Dad. 'I was Captain of football and cricket when I was a boy.'

Dad had tried to teach me football. Dad had tried to teach me cricket.

He had tried. And I had tried. But it hadn't worked.

'Tim can't help being bad at games,' said Mum, pulling me away from Dad.

She gave me a cuddle.

'It's because you've turned him into a right Mummy's boy,' said Dad. 'I think an adventure holiday would do him the world of good.'

He wouldn't listen to Mum. He

3

wouldn't listen to me. He booked the adventure holiday.

'You'll love it when you get there,' said Dad. Over and over again.

He bought me new jeans and T-shirts and trainers and a stiff soldier's jacket to make me look tough.

Mum bought me a special safety helmet to wear all the time to keep me safe.

I didn't feel tough. I didn't feel safe.

I needed to hug Walter Bear very hard when Dad drove us to the Adventure Centre. Dad said I shouldn't take a teddy bear with me because the other kids might laugh at me. Mum said I couldn't get to sleep without Walter Bear. I didn't say anything. I hugged Walter even harder, sniffing in his sweet dusty smell.

Dad looked in his driving mirror and saw what I was doing.

'Tim!' said Dad, turning round to frown at me. 'Come on, you're doing it deliberately. Put that silly bear *down*. You'll be sucking your thumb next.'

He was watching me, not watching the road. An old banger suddenly overtook us, making Dad swerve.

'Idiots!' Dad shouted, peeping his horn.

A girl leaned out the open window of the car and yelled right back.

'Slowpokes!' she shouted, and pulled a silly face.

'I hope that girl's not going on the adventure holiday,' said Mum.

I hoped she wasn't going on the adventure holiday too. I wished *I* wasn't going on the adventure holiday.

'Look, Tim! I think that's it,' Dad said excitedly.

I didn't look. I shut my eyes tight. I hoped if I wished hard enough I'd somehow whizz through space and end up safe at home. But Dad was already parking the car. Mum kept going on at

Walter Bear

me, asking why I had my eyes shut and did I feel sick, and I couldn't concentrate hard enough on my wishing. Then Dad opened the car door and yanked me out and hissed at me to stop messing about and say hello to the lady.

'Hello! You must be Tim. I'm Sally. I'm in charge of the Adventure Centre,' she said.

She smiled at me. Dad prodded me in the back to make me say hello.

The slowpoke girl was dashing about showing off.

'Now you behave yourself, Kelly,' said her mum, but she didn't sound a bit fierce. She sounded friendly.

Kelly just laughed at her and gave her a hug.

'You can clear off now, Mum,' she said. 'Bye.'

'I think we should make ourselves scarce too,' said Dad. 'Cheerio, Tim.' He bent down and whispered in my ear. 'Now you're really going to try to be a big boy, not a silly baby, eh?'

I didn't say anything. Dad chucked me under the chin.

'You'll have a great time,' said Dad.

'But if you really don't like it then phone and we'll come and get you straight away,' said Mum. 'And write me lots of postcards too. One every day?'

She gave me a hug and a very wet kiss. I wriggled. I was sure Kelly was watching and laughing at me.

'Mum! I'll be OK. Honestly,' I said. Though I didn't *feel* OK. It was awful seeing them get back in the car without me. I waved like crazy. There was someone on the back seat waving back. Walter Bear! I'd left him in the car!

'Come on then, Tim,' said Sally, putting her arm round my shoulders. 'Hey, Kelly, wait for us.'

Walter Bear

Kelly had gone charging through the doors and down the hall of the Adventure Centre.

'Where's all the other children then?' she shouted. 'When are we going to start the adventures, eh? Can I go canoeing first? No, wait a minute, what's that thing called when you dangle down a cliff ?'

'Abseiling,' said Sally.

I muttered the words 'dangle' and 'cliff' and felt sick.

'I'm going to love abseiling,' said Kelly, and she threw down her bag and started miming it, rushing backwards.

She rushed backwards into me, nearly knocking me over.

'Simmer down, Kelly,' said Sally.

'I'm not very good at simmering,' said Kelly, laughing. 'I generally bubble over.'

'So I see!' said Sally, shaking her head. 'OK, you'd both better get unpacked. Your bedrooms are up the stairs at the end. Girls on the right, boys on the left. You'll see a Tiger poster on the doors.'

Kelly and I went up the stairs

Walter Bear

together. I didn't know what to say to her. I felt silly and shy. She pulled another funny face.

'What did Sally say? Girls to the left? So you go thataway,' said Kelly, giving me a little push to the door on the right.

I was sure she'd got it wrong but Kelly isn't the sort of girl you argue with. So I knocked on the right-hand door and then peeped round.

Two girls stared at me, outraged. They were trying on each other's clothes.

'No boys allowed in here!' said the pretty one, tossing her long hair. 'Clear off.'

'Yes, clear off, you,' said her friend.

I cleared off rapidly.

Walter Bear

Kelly was being shouted at too. She didn't seem to care.

'Oh oh! Swopsies,' she said, shrugging cheerfully.

I tried the left-hand door this time. Inside, there were two boys messing about with their bags.

'Hello, I'm Giles,' said the taller one. His voice was very posh and he acted very pushy. 'You're going to be in our team. The Tigers. What are you good at then?'

I thought hard.

'Um. Well, I'm OK at Maths and . . .'

'*Games*, you berk!' said Giles, sneering. 'What school teams are you in?'

'I'm not,' I said.

'You're not in *anything*? Oh great!' said Giles sarcastically. 'We've got three girls, old Fatso here, and *you*.'

The fat boy was sprawling on his bed, eating a biscuit.

'Less of the Fatso, *Piles*,' he said, munching.

I giggled. I know what piles are. My dad had them once.

The fat boy giggled too. 'Hi, I'm Biscuits,' he said. 'What's your name, then?'

'Tim,' I said, putting my bag down on the bed next to Biscuits.

'Not *that* one! That's my bed,' said Giles, knocking my bag on to the floor.

'Your bed's that one over there,' said Biscuits. 'We're supposed to get unpacked. They're going to ring a bell when it's teatime. I can't wait, I'm starving.'

He unwrapped another biscuit and started serious munching again. Giles unzipped a tennis racquet and started swinging it wildly in the air, practising his serve.

I started unpacking all my stuff. My T-shirts and pyjamas smelt all clean and flowery of home. I had to bend over my bag so that Giles and Biscuits

11

wouldn't see my watery eyes.

Then I felt a sudden bang on the head.

'Watch out!' I squeaked.

'Sorry. Just practising,' said Giles. 'Oh goodness, you're not blubbing, are you? I hardly touched you.'

I sniffed hard.

'Have you brought your tennis racquet then?' Giles asked.

I started to worry some more.

'I thought they were meant to provide all the racquets and that,' I said.

'That's right,' said Biscuits. He quietly passed me a tissue. It was a bit chocolatey but it was still fine for mopping operations.

'It'll be just ropey old stuff,' said Giles scornfully. 'I've brought my own equipment.'

He started rifling through his bags, showing us. It all looked brand new and very expensive.

'I've brought my own equipment too,' said Biscuits, grinning. He nudged me and pulled open a big picnic bag. I saw bags and bags of biscuits, crisps, apples, sweets and cans of cola.

'Yummy,' I said.

Biscuits rubbed his tummy.

Giles sighed in a superior manner.

'I've brought one bit of equipment,' I said, showing him my safety helmet. I knew it was a mistake as soon as I'd got it out. Especially as Mum had painted TIM in bright pink letters on the front.

Giles did a deliberate double-take.

'What's that, then?' he said. Though of course he knew.

'Well. It's a safety helmet,' I said.

'I see,' said Giles. 'When are you going to wear it then?'

'When I'm . . . when . . .' my voice tailed away.

Giles was serving madly and I had to dodge sharpish.

Walter Bear

'When little baby diddums is playing tennis?' Giles jeered. 'In case he gets banged on the bonce, is that it?'

I pretended to ignore him. I wanted to keep well out of Giles's way so I went over to the wardrobe and put all my stuff away. Then I hunched up on my bed and wrote my first postcard.

Biscuits offered me a bite of his biscuit while I was writing it. The biscuit was a bit slurpy and soggy, but it was still nice of him.

I added a P.S. to my first postcard.

P.S. But I have got a friend called Biscuits.

Me playing Triangles

POST CARD

Dear Mum and Dad
I am having a
Truly Terrible Time.
WHY won't you come and
take me home ??????

With love from
Tim

Mr and Mrs R. Parsons,
10 Rainbow Street,
Didcot,
Oxon

CHAPTER TWO

That first evening at the Adventure Centre was awful. Awful awful awful.

Well. Tea was OK. We had beef-burgers and chips and peas. There was tomato sauce on the table. Biscuits and I messed about, pretending the tomato sauce was blood. The pretend started to get a bit real and I stared at the scarlet pool all over my plate and decided I wasn't really hungry any more.

It didn't matter though. Biscuits ate my tea as well as his own.

We sat with Giles. Kelly came and squashed in beside us too. She said hi to me. Giles thought she was my girlfriend!!!

Jake came and talked to us at tea. Jake was our Special Helper. He was tall and sporty and good-looking. All the girls were crazy about him because he looked like some pop star.

I thought he might be a bit bossy and big-headed, but he talked to me just

like a friend. I didn't want to be in any stupid team but if I *had* to be in a team then I was very glad it was Jake's team. The Tigers.

G-r-r-r-r-r-r-r-r-r-r-r-r-r-r-r-r-r-r-r-rr-r-r-r-r-r.

That's the Tiger Grand Roar.

There were six of us. Giles and Biscuits and me. And Kelly. And Laura and Lesley. They were the girls in Kelly's bedroom. She said they weren't much fun. They just went whisper whisper, giggle giggle. They left Kelly out of things. But she didn't care. Kelly's the sort of girl who doesn't care about anything.

She doesn't even mind if people think her a *baby*. She had this little Troll doll with purple hair. Kelly made the little Troll 'talk' in a tiny voice.

17

I often make Walter Bear talk to me. His voice is quite growly. But friendly.

I wished and wished I had Walter with me at the Adventure Centre.

The Tigers had to help clear up after tea. We were on kitchen duties. We all moaned because we got lumbered. The Lions didn't have to clear up. Or the Panthers. Or the Cheetahs.

Kelly said she wanted to be a Cheetah and then she could cheat.

Biscuits said he wanted to be a Lion and then he could lie.

So *I* said I wanted to be a Panther so I could pant. And I made funny panting noises. Biscuits laughed and started panting too. So did Kelly. And even Giles joined in.

Laura and Lesley thought we'd all gone nuts.

I started to wonder if it might be fun to be on an adventure holiday. But *then* we all had to go outside and play these terrible games.

I hate games at school.

I hate games in the garden at home.

I hate games on the beach on holiday.

I knew I would hate hate hate games here.

We were all made up with face-paints to look like tigers (orange with black stripes) . . .

or lions (yellow) . . .

or panthers (black) . . .

or cheetahs (beige with black spots).

Laura and Lesley mucked about with the face-paints, making themselves look like grown-up ladies.

Giles made a fuss at first, saying he didn't want his face painted because it was stupid and cissy.

I didn't mind having my face painted. Though it tickled a bit. But I minded terribly when Jake and Sally and the others started setting up posts and handing out balls and bats.

It was a new game. Triangles. A bit like Rounders. We play Rounders at school. I hate it. I'm useless.

'I can't catch,' I said privately to Biscuits.

'I can't flipping *run*,' said Biscuits.

'I can run, I can catch,' said Kelly.

She wanted to be the bowler and so did Giles so there was an argument.

Jake said *he* was the bowler. They had to be fielders. And he picked Laura and Lesley and me to man the posts.

Laura and Lesley giggled.

'*Wo*man the posts,' they said.

I didn't say anything at all at first. I was too worried. Especially when Jake told me to be first post.

I swallowed hard.

'Excuse me, Jake,' I squeaked.

'Yes, Tim?'

'I—I don't want to be first post.'

'Why's that, eh?' said Jake.

'I can't catch,' I explained.

'Well, just do your best,' said Jake. Giles was sighing and looking impatient.

'*I'd* better be first post,' he said.

'No, we'll give Tim a go,' said Jake. 'We're going to keep changing round

anyway. Come on, let's get cracking.'

Jake bowled to the first Lion batter. They gave it a tap and then started running. Laura grabbed the ball and threw it to me.

'Here, Tim, catch!' she shouted.

I tried.

I really did.

Dad always yells at me to watch the ball.

I watched it go sailing past my cupped hands.

'He's missed it!' Giles yelled.

'Tim!' said Laura.

'Tim!' said Lesley.

'Tim!' said Kelly.

'Never mind, Tim,' said Jake. 'Next time, eh?'

I hoped and hoped and hoped I might do better next time.

I didn't.

Or the next time.

Or the next.

Or the next.

Or the next.

It was so awful. No-one else was as useless as me.

Biscuits couldn't run very fast at all

but he was good at catching and he could hit hard too.

I couldn't hit hard when it was our turn to bat.

I couldn't hit the ball at all.

I was the worst at games. They all started shouting at me. Teasing me. Saying stuff.

When the games were over at last I ran into the Centre and had a bit of a cry by myself locked in the toilets. Then I remembered the phone in the hall.

I didn't have any change on me but I reversed the charges. I got through to Mum.

I started telling her how awful it was and I asked her to come right that minute. She said she would but then Dad started talking too. He kept asking me *why* it was so awful. So I said about them all shouting at me. And Dad said I was making a fuss about nothing. I said I still wanted them to come and get me like they promised. *But you can't always trust your parents.*

Especially your dad.

He said I should see how I felt

22

tomorrow. He wasn't going to come and fetch me tonight. No matter what.

'But you said you'd come and get me if I didn't like it,' I said. 'I don't want to see how I feel tomorrow. It's not *fair*. I didn't want to come here in the first place.'

I was in the middle of saying all this—and a bit more—when Biscuits came along the hall and sort of hovered. So I sniffed a lot and said I'd phone again tomorrow.

'You OK?' said Biscuits as I put the phone down.

I nodded and blew my nose.

Biscuits looked bigger than ever, his sweatshirt straining. He saw me staring.

'Want to see what I've got?' he said, patting his much vaster tummy.

He suddenly gave birth to a big tin of

golden syrup.

I laughed, even though I was still a bit snuffly.

Biscuits prized the lid open and stuck in his finger. He licked appreciatively.

'Yum yum yum. Here.' He held out the tin. 'You can share it if you like.'

We were very sticky indeed by bedtime. I wished we didn't have to share a room with Giles. It would have been great if it had just been Biscuits and me. But Giles kept going on and on about how hopeless we were at games and how Mega-Great he was at absolutely everything.

He insisted on demonstrating too. Especially his judo. He had me in this armlock that was horribly painful but Biscuits started waddling round the bedroom in his underpants, flexing his muscles.

'*I* do sumo wrestling, right?' he said, beating his chest. 'So *you'd* better watch your step, Piles.'

'You look more like a gorilla than a wrestler,' said Giles, but he let go of me.

Biscuits did a *wondrous* gorilla impersonation, making very loud gorilla noises.

I did a gorilla impersonation too.

Giles joined in.

We were all three strutting about and thumping our chests, bellowing, when Jake came barging into the bedroom.

'Hey, hey! Calm down, you lot. You're like a lot of monkeys at a zoo,' said Jake.

'Exactly!' I said.

'Hum hum. Me want banana,' said Biscuits, still being a gorilla.

'You're going to explode one day, Biscuits,' said Jake. 'Come on, into bed, you lot.'

'What are we doing tomorrow, Jake?' Giles asked.

'We're going for a bit of a climb—and then it's abseiling,' said Jake.

'Great!' said Giles, jumping up and down.

'*Not* so great,' said Biscuits, pretending to pass out on to his bed.

'Utterly ungreat,' I said.

My heart had started thumping again. Jake saw my face.

'It *is* great, fellows, really,' said Jake. 'Come on, lie down now.'

'Just got to get something,' said Giles, haring over to his bag.

He dug deep . . . and came out with a teddy bear. Giles's bear had a stitched nose stuck right up in the air and a sneery mouth.

'Old teddy, eh?' said Jake.

'He's not any old teddy, he's Sir Algernon Honeypot,' said Giles.

'Well, settle down with his sirship, then,' said Jake.

Biscuits was rootling about in his bag now.

'Biscuits! No more food, do you hear me?' said Jake.

'I'm just getting Dog Hog,' said Biscuits.

'Who?' said Jake.

Biscuits produced a long browny-pink knitted creature with floppy limbs and a curly tail. Biscuits made it prance about his bed.

'We can't work out if he's a dog or a pig. My granny knitted him and she's not very great at knitting actually,' said Biscuits.

Jake looked at me.

'Have you got your teddy, Tim?'

I just shook my head. I couldn't say a thing.

I got into bed and pulled the sheets over my head. My arms felt so *empty* without Walter. And no-one would have laughed at me or called me a baby for having a cuddly toy.

I wanted my Walter Bear *so* much.

I don't know when I went to sleep.

I kept waking up in the night.

And then it was suddenly day, and Jake was in our bedroom again, telling us to rise and shine. We were going up in the hills straight after breakfast.

Abseiling!

CHAPTER THREE

It took ages and ages to get up to the top of the hill. And all the way up I kept thinking about what it would be like coming *down*.

The others raced ahead, desperate to get there first.

I was jolly determined to be last.

Jake kept yelling to Biscuits and me to hurry up. We went as slowly as possible. And then even slower. And then we slowed almost to a standstill.

'Come *on*, you guys! We're all waiting!' Jake shouted.

He had the others gathered round ready to learn about abseiling. Biscuits and I had to gather too, puffing and panting.

It was like being on the edge of the world. I took one look at the steep drop and started shaking. Kelly and Giles were pushing and shoving each other, arguing about who had got to the top first. They didn't even seem to notice that if they took six steps the

wrong way they'd be pushing and shoving in thin air.

'Hey, hey! No messing around now,' said Jake. 'This is the serious bit. OK. Abseiling for beginners!'

He got all the ropes out of his backpack.

'Who's going to go first?'

'Me! Me!' said Giles.

'No, me! Pick me, Jake. *Please*,' said Kelly.

'You two are always first,' said Jake.

He put his arm round Laura and Lesley, who were hanging on to each other.

'How about you, Laura? Or Lesley?' said Jake.

'Lesley can go first,' said Laura.

'No, *you* can go first, Laura,' said Lesley.

Jake laughed. Then he looked at me.

'How about you, Tim?'

'No!' I squeaked.

Biscuits suddenly stepped forward.

'I'll have a go,' he said.

We all stared at him, stunned.

'Great!' said Jake, giving him a pat on the back. 'OK. Come and step into the harness, Biscuits.'

'That's going to be a bit of a squeeze!' said Giles.

'Why do the boys always go first? It's not fair,' said Kelly.

'You lot pipe down,' said Jake. Watch carefully and listen.' He was helping Biscuits get the ropes sorted around him. 'We'll hitch this up and tighten it . . .'

'It's tight already,' said Giles.

'Giles! Shut it!' said Jake. 'Now, we tie up all the buckles and clip this gadget here—tighten it up, see, so it can't be opened. That means you can't fall out.'

'Are you sure?' said Biscuits.

He was starting to sound as if he was regretting his decision. He shifted from one foot to the other, helplessly trussed up like a turkey.

'I'm one hundred per cent certain, pal,' said Jake. 'Now, you go down at your own pace —'

Biscuits screwed up his face.

'What if I get dizzy?'

'Any time you want to stop you just pull the ropes apart. OK? Now, I'll just secure myself, right. And then we're ready for your big moment, Biscuits.'

'Good luck, Biscuits. I think you're a hero,' I said earnestly.

Biscuits beamed at me—though his teeth had started chattering.

'OK. Start walking backwards towards the edge, Biscuits,' said Jake. 'Er. This is when it starts to get a bit...' Biscuits wavered.

Even Giles and Kelly looked relieved that they weren't going first now. The thought of stepping backwards into space made my legs tremble inside my tracksuit.

'You'll be fine, I promise,' said Jake. 'When you get to the edge stick your bottom out, legs and feet at right angles to the cliff—and don't let go of the rope! Especially not with your left hand. You walk yourself down. You're in control. Your bodyweight helps you down.'

'Then Biscuits' bodyweight is going to whizz him down mega-fast,' said Kelly.

'Shut up, Kelly,' said Jake. 'Come on, Biscuits. Over you go. I'll buy you a chocky biscuit for going first, OK?'

'How about a huge great *bag* of biscuits?' said Biscuits.

He started shuffling backwards to the edge—and then—OVER IT!

'That's it. Good boy!' said Jake 'Don't let go with your right hand Down you go. Easy does it. Great Absolutely perfect! One foot after the other. Are you watching, kids? Biscuits is doing a grand job.'

I couldn't watch. But everyone suddenly cheered—which meant Biscuits had made it right to the bottom of the cliff.

I didn't dare look all the way down but I shouted 'Well done, Biscuits,' into the wind.

'There! I told you it was easy,' said Jake, hauling the ropes and harness back after Biscuits had unscrewed himself. 'OK, Tim. You next.'

'No!'

'Yes,' said Jake, coming over to me.

'No,' I said.

'You've all got to go sooner or later,' said Jake.

'Later,' I insisted.

'No. Sooner,' said Jake. 'Get it over with.'

'I can't,' I said.

'Yes you can, Tim,' said Jake, holding my hand.

'He's scared,' said Giles.

'We all get scared,' said Jake. 'Especially the first time.' He bent down and looked me straight in the eye. 'But you'll see it's easy, Tim. Trust me. Now. Into the harness.'

I found I was being strapped in before I could get away. Jake was telling me things about this rope in this hand, that rope in that, but the wind was whipping his words away. I couldn't listen properly anyway. There was just this roaring inside my head.

'Don't let go of the rope, right?' said Jake.

I felt as if my head was going to burst right out of my personalized safety helmet.

This couldn't be real. It couldn't be happening to me. If I closed my eyes maybe it would all turn into a nightmare and then I'd wake up in bed at home with Walter Bear.

'Tim?' said Jake. 'Open your eyes! Now, your pal Biscuits is down there waiting for you. Come on. Start backing towards the edge.'

I backed one step. Then another. Then I stopped.

'I can't!'

'Yes you can,' said Jake. 'You'll see. Over you go. Don't worry. You can't fall. You just have to remember, you *don't* let go of the rope.'

I stared at him and started backing some more. Then my heels suddenly lost contact with the ground. I slipped backwards and suddenly . . . there I was! Suspended. In mid-air.

'Help!'

I reached forward, desperate.

I had to hang on to something.

I grabbed at the rock.

I let go of the rope!

Suddenly I was sliding backwards, backwards, backwards.

I screamed.

I caught hold of the rock, though my fingers bent right back. I clung to it, sobbing.

I heard them shouting up above me.

'He's fallen!'

'He's let go of the rope.'

'I *knew* he would!'

'Trust Tim to blow it.'

'He's *stuck*.'

'Don't stop, Tim!' Biscuits called from underneath me.

I turned my head and tried to look at him. The whole world started swerving and swooping. Biscuits seemed a tiny blob millions and millions of miles below me. I was hanging by my hands in whirling space.

'Help!'

'It's OK, Tim. Don't panic,' Jake called down.

'Don't panic, Tim, don't panic!' Kelly yelled. 'He's panicking, isn't he, Jake?'

'Sh, Kelly. All of you. Just back off, eh?' Jake said. 'Now. Tim. Listen. You've let go of the rope.'

'I know!'

'But it's OK. You can't fall. You're safe, I promise.'

'I don't feel safe. I feel *sick*.'

Well, you can get yourself down in a couple of ticks. All you need to do is grab hold of the rope.'

'How???'

'Just let go of the rock and—'

'I can't!' Was Jake crazy? The rock was the only thing stopping me swinging through space. I *couldn't* let go.

'You're safely strapped into your harness,' Jake called. 'You don't need to clutch the rock. You've just got to take hold of the rope and then you're back in business. See the rope? Tim! Open your eyes!'

'I can't look down.'

'Look up. At me,' said Jake.

I tilted my head and dared peep out between my eyelashes. Jake was leaning right over the edge, not too terribly far away. He gave me a thumbs-up sign.

'That's the ticket. Now. It's OK. Have a little rest if you like. It's not so bad now, is it?'

'Yes!'

'You can dangle there all day if you really want,' said Jake.

'No!'

'Or you can get hold of that old rope and walk yourself down, one foot at a time, easy-peasy. Mmm?'

I peered up at him.

'Can't you pull me up?' I begged.

'We're trying to get you down, pal, not up!' said Jake. 'You can do it. You're being ever so brave.'

He had to be joking!

'Stay there long enough and you'll get such a head for heights you'll become a trapeze artist,' said Jake.

'I don't think!'

'So just reach out—' Jake urged.

I thought about it. My fingers were hurting terribly. My hands were so scratched and sore. I *couldn't* hang there for ever. Maybe if I let go and grabbed the rope I *could* get down. So I loosened my grip, I reached out suddenly, I tried to grab . . .

I swung round and it was so scary I shut my eyes and caught hold of the rock all over again.

I heard the others groaning. But Jake didn't give up on me.

'Nearly. Try again. Go on.'

So I tried again. I reached out. I made another grab at the rope. My hand was sticky with sweat but I got it—I held on to it—I had it safe!

'Well done!' Jake called. 'There! I knew you could. Just keep hanging on to it this time, eh? Now walk yourself down. One step.'

I tried to move my feet. They were numb inside my boots. I made a teeny-tiny mouse-move downwards.

'Great!' said Jake. 'Now another step.'

My other leg moved. And I moved too. I was going down.

'We're back in business,' said Jake. 'There we go. That's it. You're getting the hang of it now.'

'I'm doing it!' I said, stepping myself down through space.

'That's right. You're doing it, Tim,' Jake called. 'You're nearly halfway down. Doing just great. Carry on. Nice and easy. Good boy. Well done.'

'I'm doing it,' I mumbled. 'I'm doing it. I'm doing it. It's awful. But I'm doing it!'

'Come on, Tim!' Biscuits called up at me. He sounded much nearer now. 'You're nearly there!'

I carried on, quicker and quicker— and then suddenly I was at the bottom and Biscuits gave me such a thump on the back to congratulate me that I very nearly fell over.

'You did it, you did it, you did it!' Biscuits sang.

Jake was cheering me from right up at the top of the rock.

'Well done, Tim! It wasn't so bad, was it? Do you want another go, eh?'

I shook my head so hard my helmet wobbled.

'Never ever *ever* again!'

All the others managed it without making a fuss. Giles was especially good at it. I knew he would be.

He went on and on and on at me going back to the Centre.

'You were so *scared*!' he said. 'You just dangled there. And you *cried*! Boo hoo, boo hoo, little baby.'

He kept pushing and punching me too, when he thought Jake wasn't watching. Really hard.

*   *   *

After tea Jake asked me to help him look for lost balls in the garden. Just him and me.

I found a red ball right in the middle of the roses. Jake was pleased with me.

'Well done, Tim.' He patted me on the back. His hand stayed on my

shoulder. 'You're finding it a bit tough at the moment, aren't you, Tim?'

'They keep teasing me, saying I'm scared. Well, it's mostly one person in particular. In my bedroom. The one who isn't Biscuits.'

Jake sat down and I did too.

'Giles?' said Jake, throwing the red ball at me.

'Giles!' I said, sighing, catching the ball.

'You caught it!' said Jake.

I threw the ball back. He threw it to me. I caught it each time. But Jake was giving me very easy throws.

'You could try standing up to him,' Jake said, bouncing the ball.

'Hmm!' The ball skidded into the roses again and I went to fetch it. I found a little' wiggly worm too. It almost got run over by the ball, but not quite. I stroked it very gently.

'I'm like this little worm,' I said, holding it in my hand. 'And Giles is like a great big blackbird. Going peck peck peck at me.'

Jake seemed surprised that I liked worms so I told him about this pet worm I had once called William. I filled a shoe-box with earth and made him a special Wormotel but then Mum made a fuss and I had to empty the shoe-box into the garden—and William got emptied out too.

'I'll tell you a secret, Tim,' said Jake.

Jake said he was scared of worms! Always, ever since he was a little boy. And all the other boys teased him and threw worms at him to make him squeal.

'So one day I thought this is nuts. I made myself pick up a worm and I threw it right back. And it was OK after that.'

I wondered whether Giles was scared of worms.

Jake said everyone's scared of something. Mice. The dark. Wetting the bed!

I held the wiggly worm out and he squealed and made out he was dead scared. But he was only kidding.

'I think you've been kidding all along, Jake,' I said. 'To make me feel better.'

Jake laughed and said I was amazing at sussing things out.

I've sussed out one thing. I know what my friend Biscuits is scared of. Running out of biscuits!

POST CARD

Dear Mum and Dad
I went abseiling !!!
I didn't like it. (Understatement
of the century.) I let go of the
rope and was in MORTAL DANGER.
But I managed to grab it again.
I survived. Just.

        With love from
                Tim

P.S. It's canoeing today. I could
still drown.

Mr and Mrs R. Parsons,
10 Rainbow Street,
        Didcot,

        Oxon

CHAPTER FOUR

Biscuits and I teamed up for the canoe race. Biscuits sat at the front. Our canoe tipped forwards. We swopped round which was *exceedingly* difficult. We got a bit wet in the process, but eventually I was squashed in the front and Biscuits sat behind me. Our canoe tilted backwards. We decided to put up with it. We agreed not to take the canoe race too seriously.

Giles and Kelly took it very seriously indeed. Jake had paired them up in one canoe. Giles stuck his nose in the air at the thought of sharing with Kelly. Kelly *held* her nose at the thought of sharing with Giles. But they made a very speedy pair and they were soon racing ahead through the water. Laura and Lesley were nippy too, paddling away like crazy.

'Come *on*, you Tigers!' Giles yelled, craning back at us.

There were just two huge Panthers ahead of Giles and Kelly. They had

Theresa

arm muscles like cannon balls and were way out in front. Giles and Kelly paddled frantically, desperate to catch them up.

'Nutters!' said Biscuits, wiping his brow 'Phew! I don't think much of this canoeing lark, do you, Tim?'

'Yeah. This isn't my idea of fun,' I said, paddling hard.

'You can say that again,' said Biscuits.

'This isn't my idea of fun,' I said.

'You can say that again,' said Biscuits.

'This isn't my idea of fun,' I said, cracking up laughing.

'You can say that again,' said Biscuits, spluttering.

We were soon laughing so much we nearly capsized our canoe.

Giles and Kelly were getting nearer and nearer the mighty Panthers. They drew close, maybe too close. The Panthers went a bit wobbly—and suddenly Giles and Kelly were ahead.

'We're in front!' Giles yelled triumphantly.

'We are the champions!' Kelly sang, and she took something small out of her pocket and gave a victory wave.

She waved a little too vigorously. The small something flew through the air and did a swallow dive into the river.

Kelly screamed.

'Theresa! Come back! You can't swim!' She sounded frantic.

Giles was growing frantic too. He was shouting at Kelly.

'Sit down! You'll have us over. What

Theresa

are you *doing*?'

Kelly twisted and turned, practically paddling backwards.

'What's up with Kelly?' asked Biscuits, blinking at her.

'She's dropped Theresa in the water. You know. Her little Troll doll,' I explained.

We knew all about Kelly's lucky mascot. Jake and Sally didn't.

They heard Kelly yelling desperately and came whizzing over in their own canoe.

'Theresa's drowning!' Kelly sobbed.

'*Where?* Which canoe? There isn't a Theresa on the course! Kelly, *who's* Theresa?' they shouted urgently, Jake jumping up to dive to the rescue.

'She's her stupid Troll doll,' Giles said disgustedly, as the mighty Panthers raced past towards the winning post.

Jake sat down again, and he and Sally waved their hands and went Phew!

'*Please*, Jake! Can't you dive in and look for her?' Kelly yelled. 'Oh, Theresa. Where *are* you?'

'Hey!' said Biscuits, his eyes beady. 'Look, Theresa's just bobbing past!'

I looked—and saw a little purple blob floating off towards the bank.

'It is Theresa! It's OK, Kelly,' I shouted. 'We've spotted her, Biscuits and me. We'll get her.'

'Yeah, we'll get her out for you, Kelly,' said Biscuits. 'Er . . . how do we get the canoe to go sideways, Tim?'

'Like this? Mmm. No. Like *this*?'

Our canoe wobbled dramatically as we experimented.

'What are you two playing at?' Giles yelled. 'Finish the race first. We've all got to finish or we won't get any points. You can go back for her doll afterwards.'

'She can't wait!' said Kelly.

'Come on, Biscuits,' I said. 'Before she gets swallowed up by a fish or something.'

We made for the bank as best we could.

'You berks!' Giles yelled in disgust. 'You weedy nerdy little cissies.'

'I wish *he'd* get swallowed up by a fish,' said Biscuits. 'A socking great shark.'

'He's going to get us later,' I said.

Theresa

'Oh, pooh,' said Biscuits. We'll get *him.*'

'To the rescue. Super-Tim and Biscuit-Boy!'

'*Dan-de-dan-dan-daaaan,*' Biscuits chanted.

We reached the bank. Theresa was bobbing in the scummy shallows, her purple hair wafting like water-weed. I got my paddle and used it like a fish slice, scooping Theresa up in the air.

She had never been a very pretty little doll. She'd now lost whatever looks she'd had. But Kelly was still thrilled to get her back. She hugged and kissed her. And you'll never guess what. She hugged and kissed *me.*

Biscuits said he was very glad that *I* was the one who fished her out.

When we were in the kitchens

clearing up after tea, Kelly tried to tame Theresa's alarming new hairstyle with a small scrubbing-brush.

Laura and Lesley sighed.

'You're hopeless, Kelly,' said Laura. 'Look, give her here, I'll do it.'

She had her own little pocket hairbrush. Kelly held Theresa while Laura brushed and styled her purple tresses.

'You're ever so good at hairstyles, Laura,' said Lesley.

'Keep Theresa *still*, Kelly,' said Laura.

'She's shivering,' said Kelly. She peered round and found a scrunched-up J-cloth. 'Here. This will keep you warm until we get your little dress dry.'

'Look, I could do with that cloth, Kelly,' said Giles, washing dishes at the sink. 'This one's all holey and horrible.'

'Theresa's need is greater than yours, Giles,' said Kelly firmly.

'You and that stupid doll.'

'She's *not* a doll, she's a *troll*,' said Kelly.

'We were winning,' Giles wailed. 'And yet we ended up last because of you and Biscuits and *Tim*.'

He dug me hard with his elbow, right in my tummy. 'Why did you have to mess about for hours getting Kelly's stupid doll?'

'TROLL!' Kelly shouted, flicking washing-up water in Giles's face.

'Kelly! Cut it out,' said Giles, splashing her back. He splashed me too. 'And then you got your canoe stuck in the mud on the bank!'

'It wasn't our fault,' said Biscuits, emerging from the food cupboard, his hand deep in a packet of Frosties.

'Yes, it's not *our* fault we're not very good at canoeing,' I said.

'The thing is, Tim, you're not good at *anything*,' said Giles.

Kelly splashed Giles again.

Giles splashed Kelly. He also splashed Laura by mistake.

'Giles!' Laura squeaked. 'Look at my shirt, it's soaking!'

'Oh, Giles, you've got Laura all wet,' said Lesley.

'Tim's the one that's wet,' said Giles, splashing me again. 'Wet and weedy and pathetic.'

'You shut up, Piles,' said Biscuits, flicking Frosties at him. 'You're the one that's pathetic.'

'Yeah, Tim rescued Theresa. He's a hero!' said Kelly, and she splashed Giles.

He splashed her back. Copiously. Laura *and* Lesley got soaked this time. So they splashed Giles back. He splashed me again. Biscuits emptied the Frosties all over him. We all burst out laughing because he looked so funny. I threw my wiping-cloth at him. I missed, but it didn't matter. We all started splashing and shrieking and then Jake suddenly charged into the kitchen and bellowed at us.

'What on *earth* are you lot playing at?'

We ended up on our hands and knees doing an awful lot of mopping.

POST CARD

Dear Mum and Dad
Us Tigers all got into Mega-Trouble
last night. But it was good fun all
the same. And then Kelly gave me a
Kit Kat before we went to bed. I
shared it with Biscuits. I had the
Kit and he had the Kat. Biscuits is
my friend. And Kelly. Even though
she's a girl.
        With love from
                Tim xxxxx

P.S. We're doing the Crazy Bucket race
today. Weird! How can you race
buckets ????

Mr and Mrs R. Parsons,
10 Rainbow Street,
    Didcot,
    Oxon

1ST

CHAPTER FIVE

I found out!

Jake and Sally had set this huge great obstacle race. We were all lined up in our teams: the Lions, the Panthers, the Cheetahs—and us. Giles was dead eager. Kelly was bobbing about, Theresa clutched in her fist. Laura and Lesley were giggling. Biscuits and I were *groaning*.

'It's not my idea of fun,' I whispered.

'You can say that again,' Biscuits whispered back.

We kept this up all the time Sally was explaining what we had to do. It involved a lot of running. Lots and lots of running.

We had to run to the paddling pool and fill our buckets with water and then we had to run—with the full buckets—all the way round the field to the slide and then—still with the buckets—we had to climb up it and slide down and *then* we had to run to the sandpit and stagger across—with

Thirsty baby tiger

the buckets—and THEN we had to run to the stream and at the other side of the water there were four thirsty baby big cats desperate for a bucketful of water. Well, that's what Sally said.

'Can you go through it again, Sally? I wasn't concentrating,' said Biscuits, grinning.

Sally pretended to clip him over the ear.

Giles was dead set on getting the rules right.

'So it's the team that fills the painted rubbish bin first that wins, yes?'

'They're not bins, Giles, they're babies. A baby lion, a baby panther, a baby cheetah, and *we've* got a baby tiger,' said Kelly. 'Doesn't it look sweet?'

Giles screwed up his face in disgust at this whimsy.

I thought the bins looked good. The Baby Lion bin was painted yellow, the Baby Panther bin was painted black, the Baby Cheetah bin was painted beige with black spots, and our Baby Tiger bin looked the best, painted orange with black stripes. They all had cardboard ears and beady eyes and the swing tops made excellent movable mouths. Jake demonstrated, making them open their mouths to pant for water.

Jake jumped over the stream to get to them. He's got long legs but it was still quite a stretch for him. And he wasn't carrying a bucket of water. But there were four drainpipes across the stream. It looked as if we were in for a very wobbly walk across.

'And the team that fills the bin first wins?' Giles repeated impatiently, raring to go.

'Not so fast, pal,' said Sally. 'The first team gets forty points, the second team gets thirty, the third team gets twenty. The last team only gets ten points.'

'Guess who's going to be last,' I muttered to Biscuits.

'But the Crazy Bucket race isn't just about coming first,' said Sally, smiling. 'We measure how much water is in each of the bins. That's just as important. You get forty points if your bin is the fullest. Then thirty, then twenty, then ten.'

'It's starting to sound like a maths lesson,' said Lesley. 'I can't get the hang of it, can you, Laura?'

'It's all much simpler than it sounds,' said Sally. 'Cheer up. It's fun!'

Biscuits pulled a silly face at me. I pulled one back. Giles pushed us into place.

'Come on, you lot, stop messing about. We're going to win, right?'

'Wrong!'

'Look, *try*,' said Giles.

'My dad always tells me to try,' I told Biscuits. 'And I do. But it doesn't work.'

'Right everyone,' Sally called. 'Get ready. One. Two. Three. GO!'

We all started running. Guess what. Giles got to the pool first.

'Come *on*, you Tigers!' he bawled as he filled his bucket.

Biscuits and I were nearly last at the pool. We filled our buckets right to the brim. We certainly weren't going to fill our baby big cat bin first, so we knew we had to bring our entire bucketful.

It was hard going, running with a full bucket. We had to be ever so careful not to spill any. Some of the faster kids swung their buckets and sprinkled water all down their socks. Biscuits didn't spill any, but he was slower than ever. I jogged along beside him, proud that I hadn't spilled a single drop.

And then one of the Cheetahs pushed past me, his bucket banging hard into my back. I staggered and fell headlong, spilling all the water in my

Thirsty baby tiger

bucket.

'Ooooh!' All the breath was knocked out of me.

'Oh Tim!' said Biscuits, ever so upset. 'That Cheetah pushed into you on purpose. He really *did* cheat!'

Giles was yelling at me from a long way off.

'Tim! You're so *useless*!'

I lay there, still juddering. I had my eyes shut because I was trying very hard not to cry.

'You cheaty old Cheetah!' I heard Kelly bellow.

There was a yell and a thump and a splash. When I opened my eyes I saw the Cheetah sprawling on the ground, soaking wet, Kelly standing over him triumphantly.

'Hey! Hey! You'll all end up disqualified if you're not careful!' Jake called. 'Is Tim OK?'

I wasn't sure. There was wet on my knees. It wasn't just the water from my bucket. I was *bleeding*.

'Maybe you'd better go and get them bandaged?' said Biscuits.

I stood up very slowly. The blood

Thirsty baby tiger

spurted a bit more. I had a truly great excuse to get out of finishing the race.

I looked at Biscuits. I looked at Kelly. I looked at Laura and Lesley, who were running back to see if I was all right. I looked at Giles. He was yelling again.

'Come *on*! We've all got to finish. You can't let us down, Tim!'

I didn't mind letting Giles down *at all*. But I didn't want to spoil it for the others.

'I'm OK,' I said. 'I'll run back to fill my bucket again.'

'We'll wait for you,' said Biscuits.

'No, I'll catch you up.'

So I ran all the way back to the pool, even though my knees were hurting quite badly. Then I filled my bucket and started the long run again, way way way behind all the others, though two Lions then bumped into each other and had to go back to the pool as well. And more came a cropper on the slide. There was a whole bunch who fought to go first and spilled all their water. By the time *I* got to the slide it was clear and I could take it slowly. I didn't spill a drop.

I caught Biscuits up at the sandpit. We staggered through the sand, balancing our buckets.

'It's like being at the seaside,' I said.

'I couldn't half do with an ice-cream,' said Biscuits longingly. 'Or an ice-lolly. Or a can of cola. No, a bottle of Tizer. Or an ice-cream soda. No, better, a Knickerbocker Glory. . .'

Thirsty baby tiger

He was off in a wistful food fantasy right up until we got to the stream. Jake was swinging the bin mouths again.

'They're so *thirsty*,' Jake called. 'They're desperate. Water, water!'

But we were all the other side of the stream with our buckets. None of the others had made it across. Some of the children were very wet, after several attempts.

'Let me have a go,' said Kelly, elbowing Giles and Laura and Lesley out of the way.

She started edging along the wobbly drainpipe, holding her bucket out. The drainpipe was only lightly wedged into the ground at either side of the stream. It jiggled at each step. Kelly wobbled, but got halfway across. She turned round to make sure we were all watching her. She wobbled again, lost her balance, slipped off the drainpipe and fell into the stream. She had the presence of mind to clutch her bucket to her chest so that it didn't *all* spill. She added a bit of stream water for luck when she thought Jake wasn't watching.

'Hey, Kelly, no sly refilling that bucket!' he shouted. 'Empty half of that out.'

Kelly sighed and muttered but did as she was told.

'*I'll* have a go,' said Giles. 'I'll have a little practice without my bucket.'

He made it halfway across too.

Then the drainpipe jiggled and Giles wobbled and he went flying too. He made a leap for it so that he didn't get totally soaked like Kelly. He just got water all down his trouser legs.

'You look like you've wet yourself, Giles,' said Laura, and she and Lesley fell about laughing.

'Come on!' Jake urged from the other side of the bank. 'Think of a way to give these babies a proper drink.'

Kelly was peeling her sodden shoes and socks off.

'Hey, why don't we just paddle across?'she said. 'I'm sure it's shallow enough.'

'Not allowed,' said Jake, and he picked up a log and threw it in the stream. 'See that log? It's *really* a crocodile. You paddle, he'll come along

Thirsty baby tiger

and enjoy a leg sandwich.'

'Well, it's easier without shoes and socks on anyway,' said Kelly, having another go across the drainpipe.

She ran to show how easy it was.

She slipped and fell in again.

'Whoops,' said Kelly, clambering up the bank. '*Slightly* easier.' She shook herself like a wet dog and then dug Theresa out of her pocket and gave her a squeeze too. 'We're not too keen on this swimming lark, are we, Theresa?'

'This is stupid,' said Laura. 'It's too difficult, Jake. It's all right for you. You can jump across.'

'I bet *I* could jump across,' said Giles. 'Look. Watch me.'

He took several giant steps backwards, revved up, hurtled forward,

69

leapt into space and soared over the stream. He staggered a bit when he landed in the mud at the other side, but he'd made it. He punched the air triumphantly, thrilled with himself.

'But you haven't got your bucket,' said Kelly.

The Cheetahs were watching. Their tallest boy tried leaping the stream with his bucket. He made it to the other side. But most of the water sprayed out of his bucket as he leapt. Lots of the others had a go. Without success.

'They're s-o-o-o-o-o thirsty, these baby big cats,' said Jake. 'Try harder!'

'We are jolly well trying,' said Kelly.

'Think of a way of giving them their drink,' said Jake.

'Well, we've all tried to get across,'

Thirsty baby tiger

said Kelly. 'Apart from Biscuits and Tim.' She looked at us hopefully.

'You've got to be joking!' Giles called from the other side of the stream. 'If Fatso stands on the drainpipe, he'll bust it in two.'

'I'll bust you in two in a minute, Piles,' said Biscuits.

'Tim?' said Kelly.

'There's even less point asking him,' said Giles.

I was thinking. It was like a puzzle game. We were all trying to do it the hard way. There had to be an *easy* way . . .

I suddenly had an idea. Though I wasn't sure if it would be allowed.

'Well,' I started.

But they were all watching one of the Lion girls who had balanced her way right along the drainpipe. She was almost at the end. But then she suddenly wobbled—and went.

'Oooh!' said everyone.

'See. *No-one* can do it, Jake,' said Laura, getting cross.

Jake just laughed at her.

'Did you have an idea, Tim?' he

called.

'*He* won't be able to do it,' said Laura. 'He fell over just on the field.'

'You try walking the drainpipe, Laura, I'm sure you could do it,' said Lesley.

'If you can get the bucket three quarters of the way over then I can reach across and get it,' said Giles.

'But you don't have to do it that way,' I said.

'You shut up, Tim,' Giles shouted.

I'd suddenly had enough of being shouted at. And I really did have a good idea.

'No, *you* shut up, Giles,' I yelled. 'Pick your end of the drainpipe up and stick it in the baby tiger's mouth.'

Giles stared at me, going, 'You what?'

But Jake jumped up and down and gave me the thumbs-up sign. I'd cracked it!

'Kelly and Biscuits, you hold the drainpipe this end,' I said, telling them what to do. 'Laura and Lesley, pass me the buckets. Look!'

It was so *simple*. We didn't have to

walk across the stream on the drain-pipes. They were hollow inside, like giant straws. We could empty the water down the drainpipe right into the Baby Tiger bin.

And that's exactly what we did.

'Well done, Tim!' Jake shouted.

'Oh, Tim! Brilliant!' said Kelly, giving me a hug. 'You're so clever.'

'Super-Tim,' said Biscuits.

'Why didn't we think of it,' said Laura.

'Look, everyone's copying us now!' said Lesley.

'But *we've* won!' said Giles, capering about. 'We're first to fill the bin—and we've got it nearly full to the top too. We've *won*! Hurray for Tim!'

All the Tigers jumped up and down and cheered. Cheering me. And I jumped up and down and cheered me too!

POST CARD

Dear Mum and Dad
Guess what! We won the bucket race!!!
and it was all because I sussed out
how to do it. Honest. The other Tigers
all think I'm Mega-Brilliant. Even
Giles. Wonders will never cease.
    I can think of another Wonder.
I'm quite enjoying my adventure
holiday now. In fact I almost wish
we weren't going home tomorrow!
      With love from
              Tim
      xxxxx to Mum
      xxxxx to Dad

Mr and Mrs R. Parsons,
10 Rainbow Street,
Didcot,
    Oxon

CHAPTER SIX

Time is a funny thing. If you listen to a clock it goes tick tick tick. It doesn't go tick-tick-tick-tick-tick sometimes and t-i-c-k t-i-c-k t-i-c-k other times. And yet the first two days of my adventure holiday went so s-l-o-w-l-y that years and years seemed to go by. But the *last* two days went whizz-whizz-whizz.

You'll never guess which team ended up the over-all winners! We did. The Tigers. Kelly and Giles and Laura and Lesley and Biscuits and me.

We got clapped and cheered by everyone and then Sally and Jake gave us all a prize. We had to put our hands in this big box. I felt something furry. We all did. We scrabbled around until we'd all got a handful and then we pulled them out the box. Six toy tigers, baby ones, with big eyes and smiley mouths and soft paddy-paws.

We all laughed and mucked about, making them roar. My tiger is a bit fatter than the others. He seems

Biscuits Tiger

stuffed to bursting. I've called him Biscuits.

The *real* Biscuits should rename himself Sausages. He ate fourteen and a half sausages at the Camp Cook-Out. (The half was mine. I dropped it in the grass and it got a bit muddy but Biscuits couldn't bear to waste it.) He also ate two burgers and five chicken wings, washed down with three cans of cola. My friend Biscuits has a Mega-Superior Stomach.

He's got a good loud voice too. We all had a Giant Roar competition between the Lions, the Tigers, the Panthers and the Cheetahs.

'Right, us Tigers, let's hear you. ROAR,!' Giles yelled, conducting us.

He roared until he was red in the face, but he'd been shouting so much bossing us about that he didn't have much voice left. Laura and Lesley had high voices that weren't loud enough. I wasn't much use either. I tried and tried, but my roars came out small and squeaky. Kelly did much better. She was squashed up beside me and when she opened her mouth and let rip I had to put my hands over my ears. But Biscuits did better. He threw back his head and *bellowed* from the pit of his magnificent stomach.

We won the Giant Roar competition too. I'm *SO* glad I'm a Tiger and not a Lion or a Panther or a Cheetah.

Giles and Biscuits and I stayed awake ever so late, swopping jokes and acting daft. Jake had to come and tell us off three times. But he didn't get really cross. I do like Jake. I do like Biscuits.

I even *almost* liked Giles that last night. And when we were quiet at last and snuggled up to go to sleep it didn't matter that I didn't have Walter Bear. I had little Biscuits Tiger to cuddle instead.

POST CARD

Dear Kelly
All right. I will be your
boyfriend if you really want.
But if you come and stay
with me and Biscuits is here
then it's a secret, OK?
love from
Tim
xxx

x to Theresa

Ms Kelly Davis,
102 Tower House,
Tower Road,
Handsworth,
Birmingham

POST CARD

Dear Biscuits-Boy
  I wish we were still having Adventures! My dad is ever so chuffed we won. My mum is just glad I'm back safe. She says to ask your mum if you can come and stay. Kelly might be coming too. Has she written to you? She's written to me twice already!
How many biscuits have you consumed since I saw you?
it A) 10 B) 100 c) 1000 ???
          Your pal
              Super-Tim

Mr 'Biscuits' Baker,
39 Marlow Road,
Market Harborough,
Leicestershire